Some Assembly Required

Un-Packing & Re-Packing Christmas

By Bruce Haapalainen

cut river press

2018

Foreword

I met a boy in band. He was smart, funny and saw things that others missed. Magically, when I spent time with him, the everyday and ordinary became extraordinary. I was smitten!

The rest is history....at least 40 years of it. Bruce has made it quite an adventure. He has taught me and shown me how to see stories and meaning in the everyday occurrences of our lives. Our three sons, Dylan, Ian and Jordan have learned this lesson well from their father. You can imagine the interesting conversations we have around our dinner table.

Bruce doesn't see a different world, he helps us see the world differently! Whether sharing a picture of a loved one with the bereaved family, giving wings to a well-worn Bible story during a message or simply weaving a tale that entertains, people love to hear him. They say things like, "You're such a great writer!" or "I wish I could tell a story like you." Bruce doesn't create or write stories, he breathes life into ones that are already there. Seeing the Bible (and life) through his eyes makes it come alive.

We've worked on this book for over a year: editing, adding, subtracting, taking pictures. It's been a labor of love for me. My Christmas wish for you is that you are as blessed by these stories as I am. Looking through these pages, may you get a glimpse of the holy in a new, extraordinary way! Blessings to you. *Jeanie*

Preface

Truth be told, this is a Haapalainen Hodgepodge – a Christmas Collage of sorts. For nearly four decades I have written many different kinds of December pieces: devotions, stories, prayers, mini-biographies, newspaper columns and then some. This book grew up from those seeds and seemed ready to be "harvested." Some of our Christmas traditions are Biblical, others passed down, still others historical or societal. May these reflections take you back to your own.

This book is no different than anything else in my life, it began, took life and was completed under the loving gaze of my wife, Jeanie. We have been together through thick and thin (lots of each.) After all these years her outer beauty still takes my breath away. And her inner beauty makes me want to keep on breathing. Her fingerprints are all over this book. In addition to the Foreword and one of the essays, she set up most of the photos, suggested many of the topics I've written about as well as editing and formatting the rest. For so much - Thanks, Jeanie!!!

Once, while shopping at a Barnes and Noble, I asked the clerk if she could direct me to the Self-Help section. She looked at me, cocked her head to one side and said, "Well, I could, but that would defeat the purpose, wouldn't it?" I'm quite certain I wasn't the first person she had used that line on. Telling you what to do with this book would defeat its purpose. Read it any way you like. Plow through it rapid-fire. Take it all in on a snowy Sunday afternoon. You might digest one section each week or take it one piece everyday like a Christmas Countdown.

Just remember, however you use this, there is SOME ASSEMBLY REQUIRED!

Contents

People

ADVENTure Week 1

i

Christmas: Eve, Day & Beyond

PEOPLE

Ruth and Boaz

One day, Ruth called to Naomi, "I'm off to seek permission to pick the harvest grain left by the workers." Naomi answered, "Go ahead, daughter." Ruth went right out and gleaned grain in one of the fields of Boaz. He was a relative of Naomi's husband - a very rich man of influence. When Boaz came to this field from Bethlehem, he said, "The blessings of the Lord!" His servants responded, "And to you as well!" Boaz said to their supervisor, "Who is that?" He answered, "The one who returned from Moab with Naomi. This morning she asked to pick up grain left by our harvesters. Since then she has worked without taking any break the whole morning.
Ruth 2: 1-7 A BEH Paraphrase

It's harvest time and even though the prices are not as high as they should be, the crop looks decent enough this year. And so there she is, trying to keep her head covered, praying that the awful desert heat won't do to her peaches and cream complexion what it does to so many with auburn hair and the slightest hint of freckles. With dirt choking her and the unmercifully active dust plugging up her breathing, she fights valiantly to keep the sweat from stinging her eyes with such malice. With more pride involved than energy, she forces herself to bend over again and pick up the left-overs from this Bethlehem field. "Bethlehem," she mutters and then laughs to herself. Not a laugh of bitterness exactly but one filled with the irony of that name. Even with her limited knowledge of the Hebrew language she knows that Bethlehem means

"House of Bread." "Wouldn't my family in Moab laugh at this thing they call a harvest?" she thought. "I have left the rich cropland of my home to be in this 'House of Bread,' picking up left-overs. And receiving precious little for my efforts, too. But I suppose it will be enough for Naomi and me to survive."

Just then she felt the eyes of the landowners fall upon her. She had heard their grumblings about the intervention of the church and state. The men of trade could not understand what right the Do-Gooders had to get in the way of the profits of business. "And we with such a poor price per bushel anyway," they would pout like spoiled children.

But the law clearly said that the harvesters could not go back to collect what they had missed. The corners of the fields couldn't be touched either, and there were traveling rabbis who saw that it was so. The object of the spring season's harvest – wheat – as well as the crops that would come later: corn, grapes and even olives, were all to have portions left for the poor, the widowed and the alien. "And I," she gasped, choking back a dusty cough, "am all three!"

"God helps those who help themselves," she heard the landowners call to the gleaners. Even though it was a general statement, she felt, somehow, that it was directed toward her. And she hated them for it. There they stood, cool and comfortable, in finely colored cotton robes that kept the heat out. Draped across overly full bellies, their fat purses hid, safely covered from prying eyes and grabby hands. Though their words stung, they had no hold on her because she was not in their fields. She was more than relieved that her mother-in-law had directed Ruth here – to the lands of Boaz. She was quite certain this wealthy man would never even know she existed, yet still he treated her and all of the gleaners with kindness and respect. Upon questioning Naomi about Boaz, she discovered that he was of the same house as her dead husband and father-in-law.

Suddenly the tempo of the harvesters picked up. They hadn't been loafing before, but now everyone was working with the purpose of people in the presence of their master. They were not moving so quickly because they feared Boaz, but because they coveted a word of encouragement from him as much as their wage. She looked over to where he was talking with the harvesters and, wiping a persistent bead of sweat from her eyebrow, realized they were looking at her. Had she been wrong about Boaz? Was he telling them a woman of Moab was not welcome here? What would she tell Naomi? He's coming this way. He's coming to me. He's . . . he's smiling. That's different. Ughhhh! Is my hair in order? How many freckles has this cursed sun added to my face today? If only I had some water to splash on this tired and wrinkly face. The master is coming to speak to me!

In time Ruth and Boaz will have a son named Obed. And then, in the wonder-filled fullness of seasons that ages wines and gives us babies, Obed will have a son. A son named David. Then, long, long after that a soul-sister of Ruth's will also give birth. A soul-sister because, as a poor and obscure stranger, she will also bear the child of a kind and loving master. Mary will have a son. In that purposeful passing of moments God's wine of sacrifice is being aged.

And though it will be generations later this humble harvest will justify its name of Bethlehem; House of David; House of Bread. Bread for the haves and have-nots; for the young and old; the spry and crippled; for both alien and Jew. And of that harvest, from a seed sown many, many generations before, we who are still gleaning in his fields, stand in awe. An awe that today is increasing, not being diminished. One that calls over and over to those who will listen, "Come to this meal, the bread of the Master's harvest – the wine of sacrifice aged in musty vats of patient faith." The gift of God for the people of God. And that gift is called . . . Jesus.

John the Baptist

Luke's third chapter begins by listing big shots: the emperor, a governor, some rulers and a couple of high priests. These are all people who lived in exclusive neighborhoods, huge palaces or fancy houses. They worshiped in an awe-inspiring, world-renowned temple, wore the best designer linens, ate gourmet foods and had numerous servants who attended to them, including preparing, serving and cleaning up their meals.

With all these prestige and high-profile people, the Word of God came to ... John the Baptizer. Luke is uniquely the Gospel of everyone: men and women, Jews and Gentiles, rich and poor, young, old and in-between. He wanted his audience (the and now) to know that in a dire time, when the world was desperate and anxious, God called on a regular guy to "Prepare the Way." His message was not just another bullet point in the world's lengthy agenda, but rather a completely new initiative. In God's time, God sends a word. In chapter 3 Luke says, "God's word came to Zechariah's son, John, in the desert." God was faithful in his promise to Elizabeth and Zechariah. It took 30 years to have their promised son, but he came ... in God's time.

If we were told, the Queen of England was coming and would be joined by LeBron, the Pope and _____ (fill in the blank with your own celeb fav) lots of preparations would be made to receive them. Verse six says "And all humankind will see God's salvation.'"

An old joke says that often people are only in church 3 times: when they're baptized as a baby, when they get married and at their own funeral. They have to be carried once, rolled once and dragged the other time. John's influence came from his commitment to Something and Someone greater than he.

Like John, let's commit ourselves to preparing the way of the Lord. What a difference it would be for the world if we saw ourselves as those who were helping to make way for something new and good.

Have you ever noticed the differences between old roads and new roads? The condition of the pavement-- or the lack of it, how straight the road is, if it's in a hilly area, how steep the terrain. All can be clues to the age of the surface. Roads change over time. At first wagons rode on rough roads through the prairie. Gradually they were made better, eventually becoming two-lane paved roads, which improved travel between the towns. In some places, two lane roads are widened to four, making driving speedier and safer. With better engineering, roads are made smoother, more level, and straighter, so travel becomes easier en route to the final destination.

Every year we have opportunities to see road construction up close and personal, whether it's a route somewhere close to home or a bit farther away. I watched as our new church parking lot was redone. The preparation took 4 times longer than the actual pour. Because the preparations were meticulous, pouring and smoothing the final surface was the quickest part of the job.

At a County Fair, I saw a machine the owner called a '44 FARMALL IH. The IH, I figured out, was for International Harvester. That old tractor looked new compared to the roller that was attached to it. Originally it had been red, but most of the paint was chipped off. Numerous rust spots had been scraped, sanded and then primed. The farmer told me it was from around 1904 and had first been pulled by draft horses.

The last feature of this old rig was a Global Positioning System. This feature, the old man told me insured rolling the ground without ever going over the same space twice. That can be a real problem, especially if you had a very large field to do. Without that little device to tell you where you are on the field or which pass you were on, you could get confused in a hurry. You'd be making crooked rows, instead of nice, straight ones. What started out straight, after turning your head to check on the roller, or turning to a new row, could become crooked and jumbled.

Preparation is everything. Especially if you start with a GPS – God Positioning System.

Headline: Nazareth

The tiny village of Nazareth was stunned today to learn that Mary, a young woman who was known to be engaged to a local carpenter, Joseph, is pregnant. A neighbor at the local bagel shop expressed near total disbelief, "What a blow to both families!" she clucked.

Others believe that the out-of-wedlock pregnancy will reflect poorly on the whole village. "People are already saying that nothing good can come out of Nazareth," said one neighbor. "This will just confirm their suspicions and make it harder on the rest of us." Said another, "This is sure to be a black eye for the whole town."

According to area synagogue rabbis, Joseph is a totally devout Jew with a completely kosher record. Legal experts agree he will secure the necessary two male witnesses and obtain a simple, private divorce decree. According to one observer, in a case like this, the paperwork can be completed, "in 48 hours or less."

Speaking exclusively with us, Joseph claimed this situation has been completely blown out of proportion. Our reporter is quoting him as saying, "I haven't had the chance to talk to Mary, but I have no desire to expose her to public scrutiny and judgement – I am committed to remaining engaged and I still love her very much!"

With a mob mixture of the curious and judgmental, as well as representatives from various media outlets clamoring outside, Joseph and his pregnant fiancée Mary – were married in a small, traditional Jewish ceremony at the groom's home.

While the couple admits Joseph is not the father, they continue to assert, blasphemously, that the baby's other parent is really God. Sources close to the couple confirm that the baby has been born in Bethlehem. Currently statistics of the day and time of birth as well as length and weight of the baby have not been made available. The child was reportedly in Bethlehem at the time. Unconfirmed rumors insist that the, as of yet unnamed, child was born in a stable due to the census overflow there.

Innkeeper

(Scholars have taught us that the story of Jesus' birth in Bethlehem has a mis-translation in it. Instead of staying in the stable of an inn, Mary and Joseph are actually thought to have settled into guest quarters of a friend or relative's house. While that may be the case, the visions of my childhood and snowy Christmas Eves refuse to leave my thoughts. So . . .)

I didn't even look up when I heard his firm, yet tired voice ask for a room. I don't know why I didn't – probably because I can't look someone in the eye when I have to tell them "no". And why should I say, "Yes," anyway? The taxation census had been an unbelievable boon for my business. In one month, I made more than in the last two years. Sure, there was a room I could have given them, but I knew others would be coming later that night. Men able to pay more. Much, much more than this poor fellow.

He was nothing more than a common craftsman – a carpenter. How do I know? Even after the long trip from Nazareth he still had sawdust stuck to the hem of his robe. When he went into telling me of the girl's impending labor I almost looked, almost lifted my head. But as my eyes began moving upward I caught the error in my books. Finally. I had been seeking that one wrong figure since sunset. After all, you know what they say, "A

11

drachma saved is a drachma . . . well, you know the rest."

"What?" I said, even though I had heard him perfectly well the first time.

"No, no room at all."

"Afraid not . . . not even just for her."

"We-l-l ok, I suppose so. It's out in the back. Feel free, if you can stand the smell. "

To tell the truth, I didn't think of them again for the rest of the night. My head was too full of other things – so much profit, and all those important people. Their heads must have been full, too, with the wonders of the birth AND the task of trying to locate a clean, warm spot for the baby. Someone said he spent his first night in this world in one of the animal feed boxes. Later I heard stories, such stories, of angels and shepherds; of stars and foreign kings – all in search of a newborn.

You're right. I should have checked on them, especially the baby, but I was busy that night.

What did he look like? To tell you the truth, I never even saw his face – never really saw any of them.

All these years later, when I think about that baby, I'm ashamed to have been so proud that I gave them a stable. I know now that what the little King wanted of me was to give . . . myself.

And I . . . I wouldn't even look at his wonderful, radiant face.

Joseph

What a night! The darkness had seemed to come hours ahead of usual that day, and there was no place to stay. I know that bringing her with me was not the best thing to do. But we were to be married – and she was ready to –she was about to be – well, we knew her time was close.

I loved her then just as much as I do now. But, God forgive me, there were so many times when I felt I was an actor in someone else's play – as if the whole story of this life was taking shape on its own and simply dragging me along. I am not a man given to uncertainty; I'm a carpenter after all. I work with stone and wood and I know what to do with them. My craft is precise. I form and plane, saw and chisel. After careful measurement and thought, rock and timber become what I envision. But as for my life, God was the builder. His purpose was sure, but for me the way was often uncertain. Those first weeks and months after Mary gave me her news are mostly a blur to me. But I remember the angel. I suppose you would say it was a dream, and it was in a way. But that face and voice come back to me over the distance of all these long, hard years as clearly and sweetly as any sound I have ever heard. You probably would imagine that a dream filled with the song of an angel would be a wonderful thing. I suppose it would have been, except for the fear and doubt. But above and beyond and through all other noises I heard, "Don't be afraid. You should take Mary as your wife."

I suppose when you unpack your creche I'm the last one to emerge from the box. Like an afterthought, or an extra piece, in an already perfect set. Eventually, I get placed next to Mary and the baby, only because there isn't any other spot for me. But I know that isn't what God intended. It was my wife who gave birth to God's Son. So, I stood in that stable and tried to keep her warm. I endured the gossip of Nazareth. I protected them from Herod and his bitter hate. I was the host, in a stall of livestock, to both peasant shepherds and foreign kings. I do not ask for praise or compliment, I crave no place of honor. I ask only when next you unpack your nativity, say a prayer for a modest man of Galilee and countless others like me others who have served through the ages. He was not my Son, but on that first night and for many others after, I cradled him in my arms through early morning hours. I hushed his fears. I held him warm and safe. The Spirit in Him was not mine. I did not give Him life. He gave life to me. So, say a prayer for me ... and for yourself.

Christ Child

Dearest Lord, thank you for the home of Mary and Joseph which you prepared for Jesus. In this season, hear our prayer that you will help us make our home a place where we can grow in faith and love. As we approach the season of Thy Son, may our hearts and homes be open to the coming of the Christ Child. In that name, we pray. Amen.

It's always amazing and remarkable to me that the Christ Child continues to find his way to us. The Christ baby comes to us, all of us, through the crooked and muddied path called human history. He comes to us as an example and symbol. May we take the time this December to share that example and love with those we meet. Worship that Child. He is a Child of truth and light. Let us look together into coal-black December skies for the star that signals Emmanuel, "God with Us," and know that he is coming for us all.

God's promise is not for a Savior of only one season or another, but of a gift that would be for all people, for all seasons and for all times. Yesterday, today and tomorrow, but most importantly, for RIGHT NOW! As we prepare top sing praises at His birth and enter a holiday and Holy Day of loving and giving, let's strive to avoid a view of the event that is way too small. Christmas is God's way of saying, "Yes!"

This Christmas can bring us to the manger of the Christ Child and provide a New Year that finds us loved and loving because we exist in the wonder of His love.

Shepherds

It doesn't seem that there is anything in all of creation deeper and darker than a black December night. And on that first evening of waiting, no one knows how many souls were out searching the deep velvety night, hoping against hope, or better yet – against their own doubt – that there would be a sign. They tried their best to bolster fading night vision, but with each passing evening, season, year, decade. A growing, gnawing doubt that drained the desire to look. Doubt caused by fallen empires and failed harvests, forgotten dreams and fugitive rainbows. And then, when finally it came, so many were found afraid – of one tiny baby's vulnerable love.

There were countless whispers and legends that had been around for longer than any one person could remember. They had heard so many versions they almost missed it when it came to be. So simple and so unusual. Passed off by a busy landlord, serenaded by dancing angels. That this was God seemed too much to believe – but not for everyone. Imagine, years later, this conversation with one of the original participant eye-witnesses:

"It had been a long, long day," said the gnarled, old man. "We had far to go and that day the sheep seemed more like mules, moving no faster than they absolutely had to, to avoid the nipping dogs. I, along with those dogs, was so tired that I fell asleep before the portion that was my meager supper could find its way into my cold, empty stomach. When I awoke it was as if our resting place was being washed by the light of a thousand lamps, but there was no oil odor from a single solitary wick. And then I heard it, 'For behold!' Now I am not one much given to things of the heart or the SPIRIT, but that sound reached into me and would not let go. The others heard it too and the first of us to regain his voice said, 'Let's go and see.' 'Go and see.' That's what he said, but we all wanted much more than simply to see. To see YES, but also to be seen. To touch but also to be touched. You become a shepherd for only two reasons – either because you wish to run away and keep running, or because you can do nothing else. That night, for the first time ever, we shepherds ran TOWARD something. Something we could not explain but that drew us – like pieces of iron to the giant magnets of the carnival magicians. 'For behold,' she had said.

And behold we did. We beheld a light, much greater than the one in the fields. A light that shone with warmth and peace. Exactly where it was, I do not know. It seemed to be centered in, and around, the baby, but it was everywhere. 'Emmanuel,' his mother had said. 'He is Emmanuel. God with us.' We beheld and left beholden – to a grip that would not let us go –to a light that would not, could not burn out – a peace that passed all ability to be understood, but that understood us.

Like the Judean nights, my heart had been black. But not so black that it could not be reached by the light of that star, not so bruised that it could not be beheld by the touch of that baby."

He was finished speaking now, but continued to look into the half dead coals of the night fire. I wanted to say something, but now was not the time. Finally, he looked up and as I gazed in his eyes, I saw light – that light – all these many years later.

The Wise Men

We traveled at night as much to face the darkness as to be led by a star. Long ago I learned that what life is about is facing your own darkness. I know that some have called us kings. Perhaps in a sense we are, but very strange kings indeed, for we have no kingdom. We look to the heavens rather than the treasuries. We are royalty seeking, not subjects and servants, but a Kingdom in which we could truly find what we have sought for so long. We were seeking a place of light more brilliant than the star we followed. It would be a kingdom which would know no end and be melded in peace. Kings? Well, we <u>were</u> received as royalty by Herod – the wicked fox. Soon we saw his plan all too clearly and made a hasty exit for the place in Judea to where the star kept leading.

When we arrived, the innkeeper was so busy counting the day's profits, he could barely take the time to grunt and point in the direction of his run-down barn. For those last miles, nights, weeks – I admit that I had begun to doubt much about the journey, and even more about myself. A lifetime of calculations and plans. Charting the heavens at night and studying the scholars' writings by day. Even now, when I think of that first day of discovery, the day when I realized it was the promised year I got such chills the hairs on my neck stood straight up. What expectation and hope fired the beginning of our journey!

And now where it was leading shrouded me in doubt. A stinking barn in this burg called Bethlehem. The whole town was amazed we had come. The father looked surprised too. I remember him trying to bow before us and sliding in what the animals had left on the floor. The mother showed no emotion at all, merely taking us to the place where the Child lay. When studying the heavens is one's whole life, you sometimes find your thoughts drifting during the night. Stars become faces and constellations. Different skies are like paintings, each telling a tale that changes from night to night. Faces. Faces are the easiest to see. One came to me so clear and so often I could almost touch it. One or two times I even tried. I saw it over and over, and I never understood why.

The sound of a rooster brought me back to this newborn, swaddled in strips of cloth and straw. I expected much of this King, and I had that right, for to the mere finding of him I had dedicated my life. I desired much, but never would have expected what I found. As we leaned into that manger, the Baby King opened his eyes and I saw his face. It was that face in the sky. It was the face of an angel, with the understanding of God. It was a countenance that shouted of the death he would one day endure, and yet it was a face filled with a peace that transcended even where we were. The face in the sky – God's face – was the very face bedded in that manger. We had brought royal gifts thinking they were worthy. And we left them, but I felt foolish doing so. This tiny babe had no need of my riches or my wisdom – he wanted only one gift of me, my heart.

Jesus Remembers

The short walk out to the hill in the backyard began what had become a familiar way to end the day. The hill wasn't really much more than a grassy mound. But, standing there, the glow from the house and town dimmed greatly and the evening sky seemed alive with light and life and promise. At this time of night, here in their special place, there simply was nowhere to look, but up. For a brief second, the teen-aged boy closed his eyes and when he opened them again he could hear that sonorous voice once more, drifting back from what seemed like so long ago. He came out here because of the night sky, but also to remember all that his father had told him while he was still alive. Whenever he came to this night spot that they had shared so often, it was as if Joseph was still with him.

Jesus closed his eyes and smiled. He could see himself standing there next to his father. He was 6, maybe 7, and Joseph was just about to speak. While the older man talked, his eyes remained glued on the sky, as if trying to resurrect every single feeling and thought from that birth night. But, while his eyes pointed heavenward, there was no doubt that his words were only for the boy. His firm, loving grip on Jesus' shoulder left no doubt of that.

For as long as he could remember, their relationship had always been the same, each playing their parts in the scenes. One never really understood the other, but early on they had silently pledged to love the another – no matter what. Both knew, somehow, that they shared much, much more than a common love for Mary.

And so it was that, following a long day in the carpenter's shop, they came here. After ten to twelve hours of laboring shoulder to shoulder and saying precious little, they would stand out on their little mound, talking to one another with eyes glued on the heavens. In that field, they stood together as partners. Gazing off in the same direction, instead of at each other, made it easier to open their hearts to each other.

As a very young boy it was from this rough-skinned man of the tender voice that the stars themselves had taken on identities. Even now, looking across the blazing sky he knew them all by name, like old friends. Too mesmerized to even speak out loud he whispered to them, "Antares, Aldebaran, Pleiades."

"But they all pale to the star of that one night," continued Joseph, the only father he had ever known. "It was almost as if it came to rest over that stinking barn. The light was so bright that your mother, awakened by the urgency of your coming, asked why I had lit so many lamps. I was angry that night, and sad. I felt in my heart such deep frustration that the best I could provide your mother on the night of your coming was a bed in with the animals. And she never complained. But you certainly did."

At this, both began to chuckle, as they always did. It was a moment perhaps only a father and son could share. And then, after a quick side-long glance at one another, the story continued:

"The night when you were born was so cold that you made every effort to tell the whole world you felt it. Your body was so blue from the night and your face so red from announcing your own arrival that we swaddled you in the one blanket we had borrowed, then in my travel cloak and finally in anything else we could find. But I couldn't help it – I kept coming over –just to look at you. Unwrapping you and counting, yes, 10 fingers. 8, 9, 10 toes. I got to see your toothless grin every time I tickled the bottoms of your feet. I'm afraid I didn't do much to keep you warm that night. To this day your mother says that's why you feel the cold so closely."

There was much more to the story: shepherds, kings following a star and bringing gifts, but Jesus skipped over it in his mind. He moved on to the end of Joseph's story. "I have been different since that night," the older man would always say. "You have brought great joy to your mother and me, and only a little inconvenience." Another smiling moment for each.

Turning slowly now he walked back to the house – alone. Even though Joseph had been dead for more than two years, Jesus remembered the story as if that night it had happened again for the very first time. He never brought any of it up to his mother, though. Like most other things, she seemed comfortable keeping the day of his birth stored safely in her heart. Jesus didn't really know if she even knew he and Joseph had talked about it.

That night, as he often did, the boy slept out on the flat roof of the little Nazareth dwelling. He always felt safer up there somehow. Up high it was as if he became part of the night sky – a display so bright that it still took his breath away every single time he looked. To fight off the falling chill of the night air, he pulled Joseph's old robe tighter around himself. Mary said it was too old to keep but wearing it made him think of how Joseph had wrapped him in it when he was a baby.

And then he felt another chill, one much more powerful and compelling than any nip in the air. For a moment, he felt like he was being wrapped up for burial. A burial that would come when – and then it was gone.

And there, on the flat Palestine roof, wrapped in his father's old traveling cloak and blanketed by a million stars, he slept - remembering the earthly father who had told him of his starry first night and resting deep in the love of his heavenly Father who had sent the star. A father whose love rested with him and gave him life.

"I Am...Kevin."

The angel said, "I am Gabriel. I stand in the presence of God and have been sent to speak to you and tell you this good news." Luke 1: 19 BEH Paraphrase

The day was not like any other and Kevin knew it. As he bounded up the school steps, the two-week Christmas vacation spread itself before his mind's eye like a smorgasbord of desserts. And if that wasn't enough, the lawns were white with frosted snow and the sidewalks and streets slick with ice. Soon people would be out shoveling and chipping, as the city's big trucks came out to dump sand trying to ruin his ice rink.

"So, I'd better skate now, while I can," Kevin thought to himself.

Today he was glad he took the longer way home. Usually it bothered him that he had to walk so far out of his way, but his mother was right. Those bad boys who smoked and sold drugs should be avoided at all costs. As he skipped and skated along, Kevin was also happy "about two other things," he suddenly said out loud and then giggled.

The first was that, unlike the last two years, there would be a white Christmas on the south side of Chicago. With the holiday only two days away it seemed like a sure thing. The second was that he could go faster by sliding so he would have more time to visit with Mrs. C before he had to be home. She would be expecting him.

For many years Kevin went to Mrs. C's after school because he was too little to stay home by himself. Just before supper every school day, his mom would pick him up when she got off work. Now he was old enough to stay alone, but Mrs. C needed him. She had been sick for a long time, and except for a nephew who worked way up on the north side, all she had was him.

Almost every week it seemed like she could do less and less for herself. So, that's how Kevin had learned to make tea, toast bagels, get the mail and even - YUCK! – change Mr. Mittens' litter pan. Sometimes he asked Mrs. C about what had made her sick, but she would always say she was just tired. She smiled every time she said it, but she looked more than just tired to Kevin.

She was kind of dozing now, but Kevin knew not to leave without calling out to her. "I made your tea and got the mail. Kitty's box can wait until tomorrow. You know I don't have school – it's Christmas Eve –but I'll be here on my way to Church tomorrow night." Her eyes were closed, but he knew she was listening. Now she opened them a little and he knew what would be next.

"Kevin, honey," she would always say, "you're such a dear." She always said that. Those were the words that always made him feel warm inside. "Kevin, honey," she began, "you're . . . "But then suddenly she paused and said, "You're my Special Angel."

As he walked down her porch steps, Kevin wondered, "Why did she say that? Who would think I'm an angel?" Her words bothered him, especially because he knew she didn't believe in angels or God, even. It wasn't really that she didn't believe in Him, she would say when the subject came up. "It's just that He let me down. It was a long time ago, but I still feel like God doesn't love me."

The next day was Christmas Eve. Yay! No school! Kevin helped his Mom wrap presents and cook and put up their tree. He left early enough for church, so he had time to stop and visit Mrs. C's. Even though it was only 6 o'clock, he let himself in and gently slid her present under the potted plant he had hung lights on for her. "Well, it kinda looks like a Christmas tree," he thought. He had carefully split the money he had left from his Mom's Christmas present, so he had enough for a box of Lipton tea bags for Mrs. C with five shiny quarters for the offering tonight at church.

He tried to come in quietly, but he startled her, and she called out, "Who's there? Who is it?"

In his best outside voice, he said, "I am Kevin. I stand in the presence of God and I have been sent to speak to you and to bring you this good news."

"Kevin? Honey, what are you talking about? What do you mean?" she asked, not certain she had heard right.

"Yesterday you called me an angel," Kevin answered. "How did you know?"

"Know what, honey? How did I know what?"

"That I <u>am</u> an angel – in our Christmas play at church tonight. And that's my line. I'm the angel that speaks to Zechy. Zanchi, ummmm...to John the Baptist's Dad. I say, 'I am Gabriel. I stand in the presence of God and have been sent to speak to you and to bring you this good news.'"

"But you didn't say Gabriel – you said Kevin. Didn't you say I am Kevin?" she asked, trying to imitate his angel voice.

Smiling he said, "Yup, I did. When you called me an angel, it made me think. So, that night at church play practice, I asked my teacher, Mrs. Jenkins, if I could really be your angel. She said she knows you."

"She sure does, child. I was her Sunday School teacher when Jenny was your age."

"You taught Sunday School?"

"Don't be surprised, I . . ." but she didn't finish the sentence because a horrible cough came on her. After he had brought her some water and propped a pillow behind her back, it was time for Kevin to go to church.

"Merry Christmas, Mrs. C," he called.

"Wait, Kevin, wait!" She called out with such urgency he was afraid she was going to have a coughing spell again.

"What is it, Mrs. C?"

"Say it to me again, Kevin. Say what you said when you first came in. What did Jenny say when you asked if you could really be my angel?"

"She said, 'Angels are sent from God to look out for people and to tell them good news.' She told me that anybody could say my line and put in their own name instead of Gabriel's and be God's angel, too. So, I thought I'd try it."

"Say it again then. Please."

"Ok. I am Kevin. I stand in the presence of God and I have been sent to bring you this good news."

"So, what do you think it is, Kevin?" she asked, her eyes shining in the dark room.

"What is what Mrs. C?" Kevin asked.

"What good news do you have for me?"

"Well, I . . . I – it's Christmas Eve and God sent His Son to us, to me and to you! The Good News is that God loves you and He sent me to tell you."

Kevin wasn't sure if Mrs. C heard the last part or if she had fallen asleep. He tiptoed out, knowing he was late but thinking maybe he should stay. But he remembered her nephew would be over soon, so he skipped off – to be not the angel Kevin, but the angel Gabriel for the play.

Church was long that night, but it was wonderful also. The children did their program and then there was a lot of singing and then the minister preached and then more singing. And then the very best part – Christmas punch (it tasted like Hawaiian punch and 7-up) and Granny Johnson's special frosted Christmas cookies. Kevin took one for Mrs. C, but his Mom said it was too late to stop and give it to her.

When they rounded the corner by her house, though, Kevin saw Mrs. C's nephew, Steve, carrying Mr. Mittens out to his car. He came over to them and said, "Kevin, I'm sorry but Auntie Elizabeth went home to be with God tonight. I took her to the hospital as soon as I got here, but she just fell asleep and God took her home."

He didn't want to, but Kevin started to cry. Steve put his hand on the boy's shoulder and said, "A few minutes before she fell asleep for the last time, she asked me to tell you something."

Kevin sniffed back his tears and said, "She did? What did she say?"

"Well, I don't understand it, but she said, 'Tell Kevin I know that his angel message is true.' Does that make any sense to you?"

Kevin just nodded.

As his Mom drove away, he looked back at the cat being loaded into Steve's car. He would gladly go back to changing the cat pan if only . . .

Kevin got ready for bed quietly and his Mom let him be quiet. He got into bed and heard her coming up the stairs to say goodnight. But then she stopped in his doorway and did the most amazing thing. She said, "I am Your Mother. I stand in the presence of God and have been sent to speak to you and to bring you this good news." She paused slightly and then went on. "The Good News is this darlin' – just as surely as God is sending the Baby Jesus into our hearts tonight, just that surely is He welcoming Mrs. C into His own heart right now."

And even though he felt very, very sad, the Angel named Kevin fell asleep smiling.

ADVENTure
Week 1

Perchance...

Ancient of Days, the only means to celebrate the special time of Christmas and to live its joyful spirit is through our dreams, hopes and prayers.

There is great power in our dreams, but we cannot forge bigger and greater ones on less and less sleep.

In truth, not just Any Dream Will Do.

We pray for dreams that might come true, Lord.

And so, we "sleep, perchance to dream"

Of a peace-filled life, not hoarded but shared with others in this world . . .

Of the realization of the very simple right of every human being to live safely in their own homes . . .

We dream to spend our nights and days in true peace ...

We dream of living a life –

With no more fear . . .

No more horror . . .

No more anxiety . . .

No more insecurity . . .

35

No more suffering . . .

This Christmas, as we dream dreams, may they rise to you as prayers, Lord. From deep inside our hearts may the visions in our sacred slumber awaken in our hearts the confidence to follow You. Amen.

The MVP

Do you remember the movie *The Sixth Sense*? It's the one in which where a little boy says, "I see dead people."? Well, this week, think about that. Try keeping track of how many "invisible" people you can "see." You know, the ones passing you on the street with their heads down, scavenging in trash barrels, collecting carts in the parking lot, running back and forth to the stock room - invisible people. Having been one of them in my high school and college days I know they could really use your recognition to help get through the day. People are people, we say, but we don't really believe it – at least we don't act that way. We are taught to "network up" in our lives, but this December I invite you to "network down." Look for people doing their best, in the job they have, to live lives of honor and sincerity. Look for people who can do you no worldly good whatsoever and be kind to them. I have always had the most interesting conversations with the most invisible of people. They work, dream, love and well – serve – the rest of us. And many of them do it with panache!

I remember each of my high school and college jobs. Among others I was a newspaper deliverer, store clerk, short order cook, house painter, restroom cleaner, gas pumper (way back when that was a job), floor stripper and garbage emptier. I learned to despise slobs. I learned to work with my eyes lowered. I learned my place. But why? I was interesting. I wanted to hear a, "Hi, how are you?"

or a "Thank-you." Mostly, I yearned to be treated as what my upbringing taught me I was. I wanted to be seen as someone who mattered, if for no other reason than God made me. Thousand-yard stares are worse than personalized looks of disdain. I've had both, so I know what I'm talking about.

The most wonderful invisible person I have ever known was my boss in the Custodial Department at McCormick Theological Seminary. I was a graduate student . . . and a janitor. I cleaned the restrooms of the people who graded my papers and I buffed the floors of other students who either didn't need to work or had more visible jobs. Mel became my MVP (most valuable professor). He looked at the Bible as if it was an Operations Manual for Life. He lived life as if it was winnable every day. He looked at winning as if it was a contest to see how to positively affect the most lives. He treated me as if I mattered.

All of this takes me to the potentially most visible invisible person of all time. He was born out of wedlock to two common people. He was a Palestinian Jew in a world that honored Roman citizens with Greek educations. He never travelled, published or self-promoted. He forfeited a divine diadem for a thorny crown and travelled from heaven's heights to rest in the depths of a feed box. He didn't <u>have</u> servants – he <u>was</u> one. Look for invisible people this season. In the clerk, janitor, custodian, parking lot attendant and all other invisible people – you just might see the

Holy! And the good news is that there are invisible people everywhere.

Is There Any Hope?

14 "'God says, 'Be listening for my proclamation: 'Soon will I will keep my covenant with the peoples of Israel and Judah.   15 In my time, I will cause new life to spring up, a fresh and true shoot sprouting from the roots of the David Tree. He will run this country honestly and fairly. He will set things right.   16 Then the Kingdom will be defended and the people in the Holy City will live safely. The city's banner will read, "God's Order Has Been Established Anew." Jeremiah 33:14-16 A BEH Paraphrase

Hope. Is there any? For us? In our country? For the entire world? Enemies and allies alike? If this is a season of anything, it's a season of hope. Or maybe I should write HOPE!?   Human history travels a muddied and wandering trail at best, but the Christ Child still manages to find us and bring HOPE. All babies bring hope – this baby brings HOPE!   In Luke 2: 36-38 there is a very brief mention of the prophetess Anna, who "worshipped night and day." She had been at the temple since her days as a young widow. She HOPED in the promises of the Scriptures. She prayed, longed, and yearned for the one who was coming from God. Like fellow prophet Jeremiah, Isaiah HOPEs for the day when God will "set things right." *"A new shoot will grow up out of the old line of Jesse, there will be a branch coming out of its very roots."* Isaiah 11:1 A BEH Paraphrase

Advent is about waiting, and true waiting requires, even demands, a very patient kind of persistence.

There is so much left for me to discover - I still need to learn a great deal about Persistence, Patience and HOPE! To many, Isaiah's stump looked unusable, its roots presumed to be dead. To others, Jeremiah's sprout seemed like a long-shot. But for those who hoped, the Messiah was God's promise and fulfillment.

There's a phrase that rolls around in my head from time to time. It's been attributed to everyone from a screenplay writer to the late John Lennon. I first read it in a book by Max Lucado. It says, "Everything will be ok in the end. And if everything's not ok . . . then it's not the end." Can we dare to be people of HOPE!? I think so – God's faithfulness has been displayed over and over again. Let us HOPE because the gifts God gives always come in the perfectly right size and at the optimum and right time. Christ is both Messiah and Herald of HOPE!

An Advent Prayer:

O Come, O Come, Emmanuel, God be with us. Come to people who await Your birth with HOPE. Come, Great Physician, heal our brokenness. Come, Suffering Servant, show us how to be faithful. Come, Prince of Peace, turn violence into Shalom. O Come, O Come, Emmanuel, be with us as we wait in HOPE! Amen

Come to Us

Father and Lord hear us as we come to You on this day of waiting and of watching and of yearning. Help us see to it that our days are filled with a rich and purposeful waiting. Through our own seasons and rituals of decorations, cards, and baked goods, let us dare to hope for what we cannot see. May we begin, no matter how haltingly, to be transformed by the impact of the promised Gift. And then when finally, we come full stop before the manger, in but the smallest of measures, may we be made holy in the presence of Your Child.

Planting time is over, harvest is all put up, field and forest lay covered with the frozen stubble of this time. But your seed is planted and growing. The eggs of spring have hatched and those fledglings, with parents to lead them, have all flown south. But your presence hovers over us, waiting for Your time to fully come …

O God we confess that we are ever looking for you in all the wrong places. We seek you among the learned and powerful and yet you find us as lowly and wretched in spirit. Often the homeless, unlovely and un-loveable are your messengers. Keep us open and curious for the unexpected ways in which you enter our lives. Teach us to notice you among the poor and stricken. Show patience when we miss your happening advent right before our eyes, but in the most unexpected places and in the midst of the least predicted people.

Lord, we ask that You come to us – as a way through the wilderness of our lives. Come to us, for there are mountains we must climb, and those mountains seem far too high. And the valleys through which we must pass seem far too deep. Come to us, for life is rough and rugged and we are tender and fragile. Come to us, lord, with a new way that is fresh and clear and clean. You come to us with a child to show us the way. Come to us in a child who is the way and the truth and the life. Come to us with a love that will mold us, enfold us, and never, ever let us go.

O come, O come Emmanuel and ransom captive Israel. O come, O come Emmanuel and ransom all of us held captive by our doubts and fears. May the coming Child Christ bring warmth to our hearts and life-giving light to our darkness.

Be born among us Lord, that we might see the living out of a peace that passes all understanding; a peace that not only beats swords into plowshares but also fashions tanks into tractors; one which plants seeds of hope, not land mines. Be born among us again to remind us how to think . . . and be . . . and pray . . . In the name of the Prince of Peace. Amen.

The Family Newsletter

At least one thing remains constant as the Christmas countdown begins. That lurking thought that touched you in August, but you pushed aside. That mild anxiety about the holidays when the kids went back to school. That full-blown panic as Halloween comes … and goes. It's a part of the holidays that can, and should, strike terror into the hearts of any self-respecting, "How can I possibly get this done before I go absolutely insane?" person.

No, it isn't writing enough checks to cover the holiday plastic. It has nothing to do with cleaning the house potential visits from white-glove relatives. It's the tough and tricky writing of the dreaded Christmas Letter. Like countless others, we receive many varieties of this literary form every year. At one time this genre seemed to be growing passé, but it has simply moved from mostly snail-mail to almost totally on-line. But still they come. I put them into several categories – each horrible in its own right. Here they are:

--The Bad-News Newsletter. One of our friends excels at this form of literary expression. From the first depressing line, "This was the year we had to put the dog to sleep..." it's a downhill ride. Then to the climax "...so with one of us in the hospital and everyone else down with the stomach flu, we got someone from the temporary agency to visit grandpa in the hospital after his fourth heart attack." And then the grand finale, an attempt at some sunshine, "...so if our court case really is over by December 31st, next year might be our best ever."

--The Nothing But Boring Newsletter. From one of our past towns comes the yearly epistle of a woman we came to know only casually in the last few months of our time there. While not long enough to develop any kind of relationship or establish common ground, it apparently just long enough to get on her Christmas letter list. And, as they say, "she does go on..." And on. And ... Not only do we review the details of life, "so how could they do anything else after a thousand names of people we don't know." ...so, my brother's college roommate met Stan in Philadelphia and after David drove down, they picked up Karen and Bunny from the airport since they had been at Dad and Aunt Kiki's in Atlanta."

--The Outright Braggadocio Letter. It doesn't need much time to explain, but we get one that is the poster child of this kind of letter. It is always customized, flawlessly personalized, and written on a special holiday paper, etc., etc., etc.

The worst thing about it are the real-life problems this family has coped with over the previous 12 months. "So how should I know what to do with all of those stock splits, dividends, and bequest checks? That's what we hire all of those money guys for!" There is also real-life conflict: "...and then the two decorators we had hired got into a big fight right there at my party. The Lieutenant Governor had to separate them..."

--The Last-Straw Missive. This is a collection of messages for which I have no single name. It's a group of letters that, without any pretense, lay out a life which is far beyond anything to which I can relate. A classic example comes from a professor I had in Graduate School. First, it never comes from the same place two years in a row. Chicago, Philadelphia, Central America, and Geneva, Switzerland, are some of the most recent postmarks. Whether describing his latest book, her marathon victory, or the kids performing voluntary, free brain surgery on Himalayan avalanche victims, it is all true and done in a perfectly factual, reporting to me.

So, which category should I choose for our Christmas letter this year? Boring is like second nature to me. "...and then on July 2, after making some Papier-Mache American flags, we were even MORE ready to go and see the parade on the fourth." How about the Haapalainens version of The Outright Braggadocio? "So, there I was at the city's multi-purpose sports complex, chatting with the mayor, when he actively solicited my ideas on how to get a domed stadium for the city." Would anyone figure out that what really happened was that I was home attending a High School football game, standing on the track around the field, when my former English teacher, turned politician, walked by shivering and asked, "This would be a nice night to be inside, wouldn't it?"

Or the bad news one, "...and then after I was fitted for the sling and my wife got a flat tire driving to get my pain pill script, our dog got sick on the living room carpet. Pretty soon all of the boys were retching and all I could do was stick out my good arm for balance and cover my head with my bad arm. We never did get that sling clean..."

Maybe I'll just tell the truth. While Professor Carl and his kin spent their family vacation researching a cure for the Ebola virus, we finally got the gum out of the baby's hair and almost solved the dog's bladder control problem. Admit it: whether on-line, virtually or by snail-mail, makes you hope you're on my holiday list, doesn't it?

Waiting Is... Hard Work

Only five bridesmaids thought to bring lamps filled with oil, the other five were preoccupied and forgot. Matthew 25:4 A BEH Paraphrase

It was my first year in college – first semester, actually. Along with my classmates, I arrived for class 5 minutes early and took my seat. And waited. The unwritten rule of thumb for the school was that you should wait 5 minutes for a Grad Assistant, 10 minutes for an Associate Professor and 15 minutes for a full Professor. When the time hit 16 minutes past the start time, I left. Imagine my surprise when I learned that our instructor had shown up a full half hour late and given a "Pop" quiz to the two people who were still in the room. I went to see him that afternoon and explained how I followed the rule and waited the required 15 minutes for a full professor. He looked at me with a twinkle in his eye saying, "Therein lies the fallacy in your thought process – I'm a Dean. For me, you are required to wait until I get there!"

Waiting is hard work – it goes against the grain of the rough-hewn wood called humanity. It, waiting that is, is patient work and patience is not a part of the human spirit – at least not by nature . . . It also takes preparation. It requires making peace with ponderous and therefore unanswerable questions:

When? Why? For how long? Is that all there is? How can I be sure?

The guest of honor is coming – I will wait for him. Take the light and the batteries, stand by the side of the road. Search the horizon. Some have no light, others no batteries. Many more yet refuse to wait for the Guest of Honor preferring their own party. Suddenly, here comes the guest. Why didn't I wait? Couldn't I have lasted that long? Extra flashlight? Fresh batteries? Anything at all?

It is Advent and all of creation is waiting. Waiting and watching. Yearning for that which is hard to see and listening for that which is so very soft it can be passed off for a gentle breeze. Was that the sigh of a baby? Did I hear it? Did you? Would I even know it if I did hear it? Waiting is still, deep, questioning. In contrast, we prefer moving, shallow, answers.

Even the creation itself is poised and waiting. Stick bare, leafless trees seem to be leaning forward on tip-roots, as if they too expect his coming. Impatiently. Mangered limbs, quickened sound like great puffy cheeks drawing in cold air past giant oak teeth. Whistling. The time is coming even upon us. Time is the companion of those waiting.

Down in the valley the creature looks up at the mountain, expecting a call from God. Somewhere in the process she gives up and begins the trek toward the summit. Couldn't wait. As promised, God, too, has begun the journey down to the valley. In the mist of the pathway the two pass – unseen by one another. One headed up to where God is no longer and the other headed down to

where the creature should be. Should have waited.
God is coming – in spades – as the old-timers say
with   a   wry   grin.

ADVENTure
Week 2

The Gifts of God

The Gifts of God would be a great theme for this, and every, Christmas season. There are many of them. Poet Ann Weems says, "The arms of God are full of gifts." They are new every morning and consistent from age to age. I believe the reason God provides so many gifts is simply due to the fact that's God's nature. The greatest gifts from God – Jesus, grace, and our own spiritual gifts, to name just a few, all come from a Creator who is never through creating. One of the often-overlooked blessings from God is the opportunity to make use of what we have been given through service to others. Each Advent, we are given the Gift of God in a sacred way and invited to live it out through shared life in community. This Advent you are able to give more gifts than you think. These gifts can be spontaneous or planned, large or small. Here are just a few possibilities:

1. Everyday Supplies. Things we take for granted are valuable, even precious, to others. Household paper products like toilet tissue and disposable diapers could make a huge difference to someone on a very fixed income. Taking advantage of BOGO (Buy One Get One) sales means you can have one and one to share with someone else. This could be anything from canned goods for the food bank to a ream of paper for your church.

2. Your Parking Spot. Say you have won the parking space lottery at the mall and are ready to pull into a close spot. Pass on it and let someone else have it.

3. A Smile. Save at least one smile per day for someone who doesn't deserve it. If you are patient and caring, your smile will brighten their day.

4. AN ANONYMOUS CARD FROM YOU. It could be a Christmas greeting or even a Just Thinking of You card.

5. A NOTE TO SOMEONE YOU DON'T KNOW.

Prayer

Thank you, Lord, for showing us a heart full of love, arms full of gifts and eyes firmly focused on our future. Thank you for sharing your Son so generously and fully. This we pray in the name of the baby in the manger, the boy in the temple, the young man in the carpenter shop, the healer with the sick and the Savior on the cross. In the name of the Coming One who was and is and is to be we hope, and we pray. Amen.

U.P. Moon

I'm from the U.P. (Upper Peninsula) of Michigan. Unencumbered by streetlights, tall buildings and people, the night sky is not only more visible but easier to become a part of.

Coming home the other night I noticed a U.P. moon in the sky. I looked at it and felt like I was home long before I realized why. It was that kind of moonlit sky that tells you the air is icy before you step out into it. There was a halo-haze on the moon, not on it really, just all around it. The overall effect was a kind of diffuse, soft white light that bathed the world in its own kind of ***glow.*** It isn't usually that cold in the rest of the world, but it certainly can be. Not too many months ago the world all around was awash in the greens of leaves and the bright splashes of garden flowers. Everywhere there was life and growth and the promise of continued life.

Now all of creation is waiting. Waiting. From the frozen ground and sleeping fields to muffled travelers out trying to start their cars. Waiting solely on the promise of a coming season. Stick-thin and bud-bare the trees seem to stretch on tip-roots toward the sun. With icy lips and soggy feet, people strain to remember the warmth of the Christmas season. All of creation is definitely waiting. Waiting for the news of God's birth and re-birth.

You can't say anything, really, that hasn't been said before about Christmas. All one can do is to try anew to feel and then live all the words, hopes and outright dreams that are sprouting at this time of year. The gift of God's baby to God's favorite and most erratic part of creation is too much to understand. Like the birth of all babies (and then some) it can only be felt and tasted and breathed in. It can only be pointed at – never explained.

This season is:

Looking at the world through rose colored glasses;

Watching a little boy get off the bus and tramp through the until then unblemished snow in the front yard;

Loving that little boy for no reason in particular and every reason in general;

The way toddlers say, "Donald Duck;"

Thinking back to Christmases both long past and as freshly remembered as yesterday;

Poinsettias, stained glass and soft music;

Drinking eggnog that doesn't live up to the way Grandpa used to make it and

Amazement I can still remember how his tasted - even after 40+ years.

This season is as soft and as big as and even easier to see than a U.P. moon.

Simple Things

Thank you, Source of All Things Created:

For each and every single day of life.

For that which quells hunger and quenches thirst.

For methods of travel and for homes to journey from and return to.

For tools that accomplish so much – both building bridges and bridging gaps.

For objects which accomplish little, save to provide a presence of beauty.

For our children, and the promise of theirs to come.

For that which is routine and, therefore, a comfort.

For surprises bringing newness with each beat of the heart and every tick of the clock.

Thank you, God of Compassion and Comfort.

Thank you, Dearest Lord.

Thank you, Source of All True Joy.

Thank you. You -

In whom the everyday is extraordinary.

Remember Not... Remember Me

by Jeanie Haapalainen

Don't recall my sins from younger years or my unruly acts; but by your love remember me, because, Lord, you are oh, so good! Psalm 25:7 A BEH Paraphrase

My High School graduating class celebrated its 40th reunion this summer. Every ten years, like classes all over the country, we gather to check in and check up on each other. Times of reflection like that are always bittersweet. The years since graduation have seen me change from an unsure, nervous, teen to a mature, confident, woman. Invariably, during the course of the party, someone will recall something I said or did way back when. Usually, I have no recollection of it. Sometimes these stories make me blush. How childish they sound! That's how my childhood friends know me. Nothing in the 40+ years of separation has happened to change their opinion.

The Psalmist says, "Remember not the sins of my youth..." I can so relate! So many of my childhood beliefs and behaviors do not fit the adult me today. I am so glad that, like the perfect parent, God loves me so much that he forgets my youthful sins. He chooses not to know and remember me for the child I was, but the person I am and am becoming. Maybe the best part of the passage of years is one's opportunity to learn, grow and change.

As a child I listened to the Nativity story with wide-eyed wonder, imagining the Baby Jesus in a

58

manger with cute little wooly sheep standing by. Through my adult eyes I see that same baby sent to change the world and bring the message of God's love to everyone. Frankly, Christmas seemed so complete then, when its meaning was replete with warm fuzzies and pageants. My faith now invites me to reach beyond the walls of the church loving even enemies. Standing by people who are hurting, hungry and oppressed, it's easy to misplace the joy of Christmas.

The best part of being part of God's kingdom is that we are loved for who we are and where we are on our journey. Ironically, embracing "mature" faith, means accepting Jesus' call to "receive the kingdom of God like a little child…" How often in life do we get to have it both ways? God loves us in spite of the "sins of our youth" but still encourages us to come to the manger with childlike wonder.

So, the Advent season can look like this. Realizing that the "sins of my youth" are forgiven and forgotten forever, brings me to the manger with a renewal of all that's right with life. With a song in my heart I can sing carols loudly and with great joy. While snooping through the presents under the tree, the present of the God baby is magnified, not diminished. Listing grocery items, Christmas card recipients and potential gifts makes it a snap to list my blessings. No matter how many times I've been, I can go to the manger over and over again with the wonder of a child. God forgets our sins, but we shouldn't forget the manger, especially those cute, fuzzy sheep!

Born Among Us

Glorious God, be light in our darkness this day. Into our deep, black December nights send a star, no send a million, to light our way and to sparkle your glory upon our longing faces. Upon the darkness of doubt, of fear and of despair, shine down your marvelous light.

We have walked in darkness, deep darkness Great Father, so we know how great is our need for your light. Teach us to reach, demand that we expand and, in your Christ Child, show us how to grow – in forgiveness, through acceptance and by the recognition that Your children all are we.

Be born among us, Lord, that we might see the living out of a peace that passes all understanding. Be born in us that we might be born anew – again and again and again.

And be born through us that we might magnify your glad tidings to this needy planet which daily crucifies itself for want of joy and lack of love. Only in that Child's name are we made bold enough to ask it. Amen.

ADVENTure
Week 3

Life in His Word

Somewhere I have the clipping of a "Peanuts" comic strip in which Lucy asks Charlie Brown, "Do you think that life has its peaks and valleys?" "Yes, I'm sure that it has." Charlie replies. "Then that means there must be one day above all others in each life that is the happiest, right?" continues Lucy. "Yes, I guess that's probably true . . . "Charlie offers hesitantly. "THEN WHAT IF YOU'VE ALREADY HAD IT?" Lucy wails as Charlie furrows that enormous, bald brow.

Many people seem to think that life peaks at some point and then *it's all downhill from there.* Such a philosophy or theology can get an insidious hold on the way we think. And the way we think has no recourse, but to affect the way we act, plan, and live. Retiring to nothing instead of moving on to new challenges is one example. Always looking for tomorrow's promises at the expense of today's blessings is another. I'm sure you can think of many more. I believe the problem probably goes all the way back to High School themes in English Composition class. Remember the assignments we had to write in those hard-backed speckled notebooks? First, you had an introduction, then the development of a plot, followed by a plot turn and finally, the big climax. Then, when you had filled enough pages or used enough words, you hung a conclusion on it and that was that.

While, I don't want to sound like a Pollyanna, I do believe the best is yet to be. And, after all, while I haven't been bumped around and bruised as much as some, I have had my share of hard knocks – both literally and figuratively. The only frightening thing I can think of when it comes to living is what life would be like if I stopped growing.

So . . . let me try a little something out on all of you as we approach Christmas. Do you think it's only for kids? Think your best one is over? Think again. Christmas comes for me now when I let Jesus grow out of the swaddling cloth in which he was wrapped and let Him wrap me in the tender embrace of the love of God. It comes for me now when I look into the black December skies and realize that He is the Good Shepherd out watching His flock by night – and I am one of those sheep! Christmas comes for me when I realize those tidings of peace have to be delivered and I am one of the (ev)angels He has chosen for the job. It comes for me and to me and with me and through me when the gold, frankincense, and myrrh which I bring to his manger/throne are my own energy, intelligence, imagination and love.

This Christmas sing a new song, chart a course nouveau, hoist a fresh sail and launch a bright hope. In the Child Christ, God keeps the heavenly promise. "In the beginning was the Word . . . " writes John. In Jesus, God not only gives His Word – but keeps us in His Word.

Merry Christmas!

Two Times for Praise

Near the end of his life Philip Brooks, who wrote *O Little Town of Bethlehem,* lay seriously ill and asked that no friends call. An acquaintance and atheist adversary, Robert Ingersoll, came to see the dying Brooks. Unexpectedly he was ushered into the Christian author's bedside. The man said, "I appreciate this, but am quite surprised you agreed to see me when you haven't entertained any close friends or family." Bishop Brooks said, "It was actually an easy decision to make. I'm quite confident I'll see them again in the next world . . . This may be my last chance with you!"

Although the line has already been used by Charles Dickens to describe 19th Century Paris and London, early A.D. was definitely the "Best and Worst of Times." Israel was an occupied state of Rome which was ruled by Caesar Augustus and his puppet king, Herod. Earning enough to make ends meet was very difficult and justice was reserved for the rich and nonexistent for everyone else. Poverty was a gateway for sickness which bred poverty which spawned ... – you get the idea. It had been four centuries since the last words of scripture had been penned and many, made tired by the waiting had given up on looking for the Messiah. For many, and in many ways, it was the worst of times.

There were those for whom hope was still alive, though. Astronomers in eastern realms saw promise in the night sky. Hope was not dead in everyone. Not everyone was corrupt. There were still constant prayers being lifted by the faithful believers and heard by a benevolent God. The Romans provided drinking water and travelling turnpikes in quality and quality that were unparalleled. Faith hadn't been snuffed out. For some, those who looked for the signs, it was the best of times.

Come to think of it, the only two times worth praising God are the Good Times and the Bad Times. Like the seasons, times change, and we are asked to ride the wave into the future. To do so requires a look from the proper perspective.

A man went to see his doctor. When the physician asked why he was there, the patient answered, "I'm in desperate need of help. I might even be dying. Everywhere I touch, it hurts. If I touch my head - it hurts; my leg; stomach; chest; they all hurt." The doctor examined him slowly and carefully, then said, "Well, there's good news and bad news. The good news is, you aren't dying. The bad news, well, I'm going to have to set that broken finger."

In that first Christmas season, God touched Mary with change. In return, Mary touched God with praise. If only, this Christmas, that would be my response to all of the change and chance of my life – PRAISE. After all, I am only asked to praise in two times – in good times and in bad.

Room for God

A family that I have heard about had a practice of learning a new word each week. At the dinner table, they would unveil the word for the next seven days and then challenge the children to use it in sentences. Eventually the game developed to where the children tried different actions and activities to show that they understood the word and its meaning.

When the family moved to a new city the kids rode the bus. Even though they weren't far from school, they rode the bus due to numerous busy streets. After they had been there a week or so, the mother went to meet the bus and – no kids! A phone call home revealed they weren't there, so she drove the route back to school with a sinking feeling in the pit of her stomach. Not finding them anywhere, she returned home and, as she turned the corner to their street, there they were! Before she could really tear into them, the youngest said, "We took an alternate route home. Aren't you proud of us?" She didn't get it at first, but then she remembered that the word for the week was, alternate. They had been showing her they knew what it meant.

Tradition is good and right. In many ways, it is what holds us together in families and in societies. But maybe we shouldn't take the same route to the manger this Christmas. Instead of getting in tug-of-wars between what we can do and what we feel we should do, maybe we need an alternate route.

The Christmas season usually starts at the after-Thanksgiving Sale-a-Thon and ends at the manger. What if we find an alternate route to Jesus? That way, instead of coming to Christmas stumbling exhausted into the barn and collapsing in a heap in front of the Child of God who is God, we can take him with us whenever and wherever we go.

It's not that we are a stranger to the manger – just too pooped to be in awe of its truth. Just a thought. Maybe we could even become mangers – to hold and share the King of Kings. Many people will get presents from us this year. Perhaps what they really need from us is a glimpse of God's presence. The Bible doesn't say that Mary and Joseph were too poor to afford a room. It says no one would give them a room, because they couldn't (or wouldn't) make room for God.

Does any of this sound familiar to you? Because I am hitting the nail of my head with my own hammer here! If, as I learned as a child, "it is the thought that counts" in gift giving, what kind of gifts do we give at Christmas time? Some of mine in past years are under the category of "There was a more perfect gift, but I didn't have that much money." Or "If you don't like it, I don't either, but I ran out of time." Or worst of all, "I had to get you this, even though I wasn't planning to, because you got me something!"

There are more gifts than you think that are incredibly inexpensive and have a one-size-fits-all feature: a smile to flash as you pass by, giving up the closest parking spot to someone else, a gift to your favorite charity, a renewed friendship or an anonymous gift of kindness because . . . well, frankly . . . just because.

After all, the original Christmas gift is over 2000 years old. And still in style!

Star Baby

December nights can be black;

But not so black as to hide His star.

Deep in space there are intense, dense quarters named "black holes,"

So greedy all light is captured - never to be seen again.

God is just the opposite - light radiating;

Direction for every human thought and intention.

Journeywomen and men still search velvet December nights longing for a sign,

Their night vision bolstered by hope but also heavy with doubt.

Doubt brought forward over fallen empires and failed harvests.

Skeptics. Fearing the vulnerable love of a baby -

Hindered by a busy landlord,

Yet serenaded with dancing angels.

That this was God seems too much to believe.

Our hearts, like December nights, can be black;

But not so black

That the light of the star cannot reach,

Us.

On this deep, dark December night - His star is rising!

Side Kick

Isaiah said (about John,) "He's the voice shouting in the wilderness, 'Get ready, the Lord's coming! Make sure the path is clear of debris! Valleys will get filled-in, and high places levelled off. All the curves will be straightened out and spots that are bumpy will be smoothed over. Only then will all people see and experience God's salvation.'"
Luke 3: 4-6 A BEH Paraphrase

Every Super Hero in the comic books worth his salt has a side-kick. Batman has Robin; Superman, Jimmy Olson and the Green Hornet has Kato. Jesus had his cousin, John the Baptist. Like any good sidekick, John took care of details and tried to set the stage for his Superhero to be, well, super. But the Kingdom Jesus comes to show us is hardly super to our way of thinking. God's Kingdom is very far from the perfection we envision. Even his sidekick had some doubts, asking, *"Are you the one, or should I keep looking?"* (Luke 7:20 A BEH Paraphrase)

Over time John realized that even though things weren't happening the way he would have done it, they were happening God's way. And often God's way requires . . . waiting. Eventually, as John's duty was ending, he said, "He must increase so I must decrease." (John 3:30) Sometimes, when doing marriage counselling, I give couples the assignment of contemplating what in their personal life could decrease some so that their relationship might increase. At first, they resist, struggle even, but eventually their lists take shape. Sadly, often after they are compiled; one, the other or both of them say they don't want to do what needs to be done to build up their life together. We shouldn't be smug hearing that. How many times, when praying, "Thy Kingdom come - " do we really mean, "My kingdom come -?" Like freshly poured and troweled concrete on a brand-new highway, we are called to straighten the curves and make the rough places smooth. As God's followers (sidekicks) today, let's help make it as smooth a way as possible.

Prayer –

We are waiting for you to be born among us, Lord. Encourage us to living out a peace that passes all understanding. We are waiting for you to be born in us that we might be born anew - again and again and again. We are waiting for you to be born through us that we might magnify Your glad tidings to this needy planet which daily crucifies itself for want of joy and lack of love. Only in Your Holy Child's name are we made bold enough to ask it. Amen.

Bethlehem Light

Lord, we too are people who walk in darkness. Help us to see your great light. We who dwell in a land of deep darkness, shine your light on us. Thank you for the Light of Hope that SHINES on the Darkness of Despair. Your light shines in the darkness, and the darkness has not overcome it. In our savage world, keep love alive so your Light of Life might SHINE on the Darkness of Suffering everywhere.

As Joseph went up from Galilee to Judea ... may our lives be a journey travelled in your grace. We are in such desperate need for the Light of Salvation to SHINE on the Darkness of Oppression and Domination.

As your angel appeared to the shepherds, they were filled with great fear. We are grateful, Father, for the Light of Joy to SHINE on the Darkness of Fear.

Glory to You, God in highest heaven, that here on earth there may be peace. Let your Light of Shalom SHINE upon the Darkness of our Anxious World.

The shepherds went hesitantly, then returned glorifying and praising you for all they had heard and seen, just as it had been told them. The Light of Wonder SHINES on the Darkness of Uncertainty.

But when Herod the king heard this, he was troubled, and all Jerusalem with him ... Thank you for the Light of Devotion which SHINES on our Darkness of Suspicion.

In the Lights of Hope, Light, Salvation, Joy, Wonder and Devotion we live and move and have our very being. Thank you for your Son, the Light of the World that cannot be overcome by this world's darkness! Amen.

ADVENTure

Week 4

Take the Bike

Not surprisingly I (and probably you also) have been thinking quite a bit about gifts and giving. The other day I heard about a little boy who went to see a shopping mall Santa. After climbing up into his lap, the boy pulled out a list stating that he wanted a bicycle, PlayStation Vita, baseball and bat, electric scooter and an Android smart phone. Santa stroked his beard and said, "That's quite a list. I'll have to check between now and Christmas to see whether or not you've been good." Almost immediately the boy replied, "Don't bother wasting all that time to check. I'll just take the bike right now and we'll call it even." In the Christmas season I'm afraid that we are all too easily satisfied by trying to receive part of the gift, not all of it. We allow ourselves to be warmed slightly by the Christmas Spirit, but don't want to be completely ignited by the Spirit of God present in the baby.

Another time a husband and wife were going over their holiday gift list for children and the wife said, "This year we'll get John a watch." "A watch," protested the husband. "What happened to the water-proof, shock-proof, anti-magnetic, unbreakable, self-winding and crush-proof one we gave him last year?" "He lost it," the wife answered. Every year I read from Isaiah: *"There's a shoot coming up from the stump of Jesse's family tree; a branch that will bear fruit because it's directly connected to the roots. The wolf and lamb will live in peace, the leopard and the goat will sleep in the same bed, the calf and the lion and the yearling will play together, and a little child will be in charge."* (A BEH Paraphrase) Every December we receive the gift and then sometime not too far into the new year – we lose it again.

Maybe this will be the year to receive that water-proof, shock-proof, anti-magnetic, un-breakable, self-winding and crush-proof gift that is God's Son, and not lose track of it like we so often do. Maybe this will be the year when we can move just one step closer to a time when the impossible seems a bit more possible. Maybe icy stares will melt just a little. Maybe more tears will be shed in joy than spent on sorrow and frustration. Maybe. Maybe we will all realize how much wisdom there is in letting a little child lead us.

Open Hearts

Unstop our ears, O God -

> so that we may hear the angel song,

> and the cries of our neighbors.

Uncover our eyes, Light of the World -

> to see the stars shining in the dark of night,

> and reveal the needs of those around us.

Unfasten our mouths, Word Made Flesh -

> to sing of peace and justice to captives and
> captors

> and challenge to action the complacent.

Unlock our hearts, Source of Peace -

> to become fit mangers,

> and receive the coming of God's Christ.

Again.

Into our world and into our lives. Amen.

Irrational Season

He will lead his flock with the strength of God and in the beauty of the name of the LORD. His people will live there in Shalom, and he will be held in honored everywhere.   He is the source of peace. Micah 5: 4-5 A BEH Paraphrase

The Old Testament prophet, Micah, even though he wouldn't use the word, is talking about purpose. Purpose refers to destination and intention. What is the purpose of this Messiah? Micah says he will stand to lead his flock, be highly honored around the world and light up our universe as the source of peace. What a great purpose! In Jesus, we have a caring shepherd, a powerful and positive mentor and an untiring peacemaker.

Our Church Covenant says we believe Jesus, "revealed God as being present among us: showing God's intentions for us, [Purpose] unfolding God's hopes for us [Mentoring] and expressing God's love for us." [A Life of Peace] Jesus came to reveal as much to us about ourselves as he did to show who God is.

The world has a long, long way to go, but God's purpose will ultimately be served. Overcoming violence, greed and many human detours, he still comes. Coming as the Peace of God. An ultimate Friend. He comes into a world filled to overflowing with people and teaches us how not to be alone. Emmanuel. God with us. With us when we feel we are losing our faith; with us when we feel we have lost our way; with us when our life's agenda of lost and found, sometimes makes it seem as if all's lost with little or nothing ever being found.

My favorite poem about Christmas is from Madeline L'Engle. She writes:

This is the irrational season
When love blooms bright and wild.
Had Mary been filled with reason
There'd have been no room for the child.

Two things to consider as we wait again for this baby are his vulnerability and his power. What is weaker than a newborn? While an infant can't feed, heal, teach or protect itself, what has more power to melt a human heart than the smile of a toothless baby? Even the gruffest of countenances melts into a grin when a baby is around. Let that vulnerability and power overtake you again this year.

Prayer

Gracious God, we are grateful for a power to transcend our own. Grant us a renewed experience of Jesus, your Purpose and your Son. In the name of the coming Child Christ. Amen.

Irrational Season 2

Speaking on the birth of the Christ Child, the prophet Isaiah said, "The wolf shall dwell with the lamb and the leopard shall lie down with the kid, and the calf and the lion and the fatling together, and a little child shall lead them."

In preparing to celebrate such a special birth we realize that facts and figures don't help us much in this season of angels and miracles. This is the time of love beyond reason; of hope without boundaries. Instead of speaking in prose, Christmas is for poetry. Every December I remember the words of Madeline L'Engle:

> This is the irrational season
> When love blooms bright and wild.
> Had Mary been filled with reason
> There'd have been no room for the child.

He came in a time when the key words were politics and economics. He came when there was a great desire for military might and a military leader. He came in a time not so very different from our own. The baby came and then they remembered Isaiah, "The wolf shall dwell with the lamb . . . and a little child shall lead them."

Carl Sandburg said, "A baby is God's opinion that the world should go on." This baby is God's promise that it will, if we will follow. Jesus is the one child who can free all of God's children from their suffering and sin. He is the one who makes his way along the murky path of human existence and emerges shining, even more brightly than the star that takes us to him, if we will follow.

Follow him through the joy and excitement of the holidays; follow through the drudgery and chill of winter. Follow through the freshness of spring, the oppressive heat of summer and the autumn, with all that it brings. Each journey begins with the first step, and this is the time to begin. Which way to go? "And a little child shall lead them . . . "

Christmas: Eve, Day and Beyond

By the Way of Bethlehem

O God, you have made this a holy night – a night of music and mystery – of colored glass and captive hearts – of light and love.

By the way of Bethlehem lead us, Lord, to a newness of life, by the innocence of the Child renew our own trust in you and each other;

By the music of your heavenly choir, make still the earth's clamor;

By the shining of a star, guide our feet in the ways of peace.

Come and fill us with a light that brightens every corner of our darkness.

Holy Child of Bethlehem, come to us. Tonight, without caution or hesitation, we open wide the door to our hearts.

Holy Child of Bethlehem, lift us from the routine of life to the splendor of a true silent and holy night. Carry us away from the extravagance of this life into the simplest wonder of your birth.

Holy Child of Bethlehem, come to us, be born in us. Even us.

Even now.

Amen.

Away from Home

So, she had her first child, a boy. She snuggled him in cloth strips and laid him in a feed box for the animals, because they had nowhere else to lay their heads. Luke 2:7 A BEH Paraphrase

It has always struck me that the very things we long for at Christmas – home and family – are the things that no one had on the first Christmas. Nearly everyone was out of position. Except for Herod (and who wants to be in his sandals?) everyone is far away from home. Mary and Joseph had to travel to the town of his roots for a census. The shepherds and wisemen (for very different reasons) found themselves a long, long way from hearth and home. And the heavenly host of angels (that's Bible talk for a whole bunch) was dispatched from heaven to a field in the middle of nowhere.

Then there was the baby. Jesus came the farthest of all: from the loving warmth of the Creator of the Universe to the more than modest feed box of some cows in an Innkeeper's barn. He came the farthest and gave up the most to make sure we got the message. That fact has been of more than a little comfort to me over the years. Whether I have spent Christmas away from home and not been able to be with family or when I've been with family and caught myself thinking, "Who are these people?" and "Am I really part of this bunch?" Despite the stress and anxiety of family, it is the place where the heart can snuggle in the deepest and the best.

According to singer/songwriter Francesca Battistelli: "Christmas is music and family in town; Christmas is Snoopy and Charlie Brown. It's mom going crazy 'cuz the turkey got burned; It's saying thanks for some gift you'll return."

Christmas can be outdoor lights strung along rooftops or roadways.

Christmas can be an inviting blanket of the whitest snow you can imagine.

Christmas is the Christ Baby of God, leaving Heaven's throne looking for a new home in "every heart that will prepare him room."

Prayer:

Loving Lord, help us be sure that this Christmas we aren't manger strangers. Don't let us to be too busy to reflect on the gift on having you in our world. In the name of the Holy Baby. Amen.

Baby Jesus

Dear Baby Jesus,

Does it seem strange to you that I would write? I suppose it is. After all, I <u>do</u> know that you have already been born - long ago, under a deep, dark Judean sky. I know what has come to pass. In that sense, it's silly to write. And it's risky. It might even be thought childish or foolish - or some other "ish" word to mean that I am losing my sense of reality. It <u>is</u> strange to write to a baby who grew to manhood and left this planet so long, long ago.

There are those who find it even more foolish to write and act as if you were present in the world now. Here we float in our own little solar system, a tiny blue marble far removed from the center of our own galaxy, let alone universe. And when we look in on the news of our world you seem a long, long way off. I suppose the case could be made that you have never been here at all. But, our persistent faith is one that hopes all things, bears all things, believes all things, and endures all things. And so, we write, we speak, and we pray to you.

Watch over those whom we hold dear. Guard those who we know and especially those with whom we share the planet and yet will never know. And deliver us all into the spirit of peace where Muslim and Jew would sit at table with followers of Confucius and Christ and everyone else; all

Koreans could disregard whether they were born in the south or north and all peoples of the world might think of their children first and their divisions not at all.

Where there is loneliness, come in a friendly voice or kindly deed. Where there is confusion, be a source of calm. Where there is anger, peace; exhaustion, rest; and where there is need, teach us to be Your arms and legs and hands and feet. For feuds that exist in our own lives, tenderize our hardened hearts that we might be encouraged to take the first step, speak the first word, mend the first fence.

As your mother Mary delivered you in that Bethlehem barn, deliver us from evil through the richness of blessings that only you can provide. With tomorrow's first light allow us to arise filled with gladness that we too are your children. And, then, when this old year has brought its best and done its worst - might we still be called people who hope in the year that is new and recall the best of what is past.

Prayer

Dearest little baby, be born in us tonight. Make us listening hillsides, eager shepherds, searching kings. Make our hearts stabling mangers in which you might be born in power and in light. Lead us, Little Child. Amen.

Thimble Kisses

In 3rd grade I had rheumatic fever, so I got to spend my birthday in the hospital – my 9th birthday. Everyone was exceptionally nice to me that day. The hospital's cook, replete with smudged apron and hair net, came down to my room to ask what I wanted her to prepare for my special day. She was shocked when I asked for creamed hamburger over mashed potatoes. What I remember most about that stay was the birthday present I got from my Grandmother – 5 silver dollars and a hard-covered copy of Peter Pan. I think that might be the only time in my life I was well-off. I had enough money to buy anything I could think of <u>and</u> I had a special book to read.

Years later, we were serving a little church, cashing in life insurance policies because, well because, we liked to eat. The pay they offered was all they could afford, but it fell somewhere south of the amount we needed for survival. "How do I look today - good for another 90 day?" I'd ask me wife. When she nodded yes, I'd cash in another policy. If I was at my most well off that year I was in the hospital, this was the year of my most dire poverty. Christmas came, and I had nothing to give my wife Jeanie. Nothing. All that pain and nowhere to turn. I spent hours each December day trying to figure out what I could give her that would cost as close to nothing as possible. If you should ever see things I've made with my hands, you'd know that was out.

Somehow, in my angst, I recalled my hospital stay, those shiny dollars and . . . Peter Pan. In the book, when Peter loses his shadow, he and Tinker Bell sneak into the Darlings' bedroom to look for it. When it is finally found, and soap fails to adhere it, Wendy offers to sew his shadow on. Peter is grateful, and Wendy offers to give him a kiss, but Peter doesn't know what that is. To keep from embarrassing him, and because she has a thimble on her finger, Wendy says, "Here," and places the thimble-kiss in the palm of Peter's hand.

That's it! How much can a thimble cost? Maybe I can even afford ten or a dozen! So, I went on line and found a woman who advertised sewing supplies. I emailed her and asked her for a nice – cheap – thimble or two. She answered, asking how nice, how cheap and why? I simply sent back, "Do you remember Peter Pan?" She did.

A few days later, 3 beautiful thimbles arrived in the mail. They were exquisite, works of art really, if you can imagine that of a sewing implement. But there was no invoice. So, I emailed her and asked how much they were, so I could decide which one(s) I could afford.

She simply typed, "One million dollars." My equally brief reply was – "You've GOT to be kidding!!!"

Her answer? "Either a million bucks or nothing. If you don't have the million, you don't have enough. After all," she asked, "how much is a kiss worth?" They were, she told me, a gift.

She must have contacted her friends, too, because, almost daily, right up until Christmas, packages arrived containing thimbles. I got thimble upon thimble. A silver tone one with dimples came from Iowa. Another arrived from Europe. It was glazed ceramic with a windmill painted on the side. I got rubber ones, plastic ones and ones made of metal. One with no tip on the end came from a tailoring company. I even received a big bag of unfinished wooden thimbles from the Virgin Islands. Apparently, the business there personalized them on request. The note said I could finish them however I wished.

I got "kisses" from places I had been to, places I had only heard of and some I didn't even know existed. All were gifts from people I will never, ever meet. Like Peter Pan, until that Christmas, I never fully knew all that a kiss could be. And we still have them, tucked away in an antique looking box rescued from a neighborhood garage sale. You can never have too many kisses - I mean thimbles.

No, I mean kisses.

Love Received

Dearest God,

As we gather to celebrate Jesus' birth, may we also be made ready to receive the love you grant us in that little baby.

Help us to find ways of sharing your love with all the world.

As the shepherds found their fulfillment in that manger, may we find Jesus in the love and joy that we share together.

Bless the gifts which we bring to your manger today that they may be shared for your glory and honor.

May what we do, and the way in which we do it, proclaim a Kingdom of peace and a Child of Light and Love.

In the name of that One. Your Son.

Our Hope.

Amen.

Tall and Beautiful Angels

Be ready, I will send a messenger, to prepare my way. After that, seemingly out of the blue, the One you have been trying to discover will appear in the temple that belongs to him; the bearer of the promise, you need and want, will have arrived,' says the one GOD. Malachi 3:1 A BEH Paraphrase

John Wagner, creator of the comic strip Crabby Road, has one of his characters comment on Christmas by asking, "What other time of the year do you sit in front of a dead tree in the living room and eat candy out of your socks?" Christmas is a wild time. In a world of facts and figures, we are invited to put aside everything except our sense of expectation.

My favorite Christmas legend is about angels and little children. It seems, according to this legend, that on Christmas Eve, tall and beautiful angels swoop down from the heavens and gather the little children out of their beds from all around the world. The angels quickly take the children up into heaven where, amidst the stars, they play with the angels and the Baby Jesus, singing and dancing at His birthday party. Then, just as the dawn begins to break, the children are returned to their cozy, warm beds. When they awaken and tell their parents of the wonderful adventures they've had, the parents (of course) don't believe them. "It was only a dream," the grown-ups say. But if they would only look carefully enough they would know the truth of their children's words. For a look at their little faces, according to the legend, reveals that the children have stars in their eyes.

Why wasn't Jesus born in Jerusalem, or even Rome, instead of Bethlehem? Why not make sure he had rich and prominent parents? Why not make him a priest instead of a carpenter's son? A world leader? A doctor? Why not? At its core, the Christmas story isn't about right and might. It is unconcerned with worldly standards. It has only one interest – us. You and me. The story of Jesus' birth, and just about all of the rest of Jesus, can only be understood as a love story. A God so in love with us that God could not, cannot and will not give up on us.

The little children's starry eyes come from their journey with the angels on the way to the Christ Child. If this year will be your first honest-to-goodness encounter with the Christ Child, get someone to travel this new path with you. Look for someone with stars in their eyes.

Prayer –

Help us look for you in every part and parcel of our life. Bless us, Lord, with a sense of urgent expectancy. In your holy name. Amen.

God's Gifts

Christmas is the time when, in my "business," I often have the most dis-satisfied "customers." At first thought, I suppose you would imagine this to be a highly successful and rewarding time for the Church, and it is. But the absolute and simple truth of the matter is that Christmas is the time when the number of flaring tempers, bruised egos and lips frozen into a pout increases exponentially. It comes from no small number of people expecting too much, giving too little, and no clue as to what to do about it. Maybe it's because God's gift of a baby, His baby, to this unstable and erratic creation that we are, is just too much to understand, certainly too much to ever explain.

Come to think of it, most of the top drawer, First Class, A-Number-1 things in life can never be explained. Felt, tasted, heard, seen, shared and breathed in--but not explained. Falling in love, being a parent, once in a while understanding what "it" is all about, occasional acts of kindness with no thought of reward--all can only be pointed to, NEVER explained. Some of the things to which I believe Christmas is akin include the following:

★ looking at the world through rose-colored glasses;
★ taking the rose-colored world for what it is;
★ watching a little boy get off the bus and tramp through (until that very moment)

unblemished shimmering snow I the front yard;

★ sitting at the table when another one says, "today was the best day of my whole life!";

★ the way toddlers say Donald Duck;

★ seeing a school yard fight end with the two "combatants" shaking hands and exchanging SWEET TARTS for a like number of M&Ms;

★ poinsettias, stained glass and soft organ music;

★ drinking eggnog...just because;

★ trying not to eat fruit cake (for more reasons than "just because");

★ realizing, to the tips of your toes, how much you can love, knowing how powerful it is – even to the point sometimes of pain – and then realizing how much greater God's love is;

★ being transformed by a baby;

★ after all these years, still meeting God on a deep and cold December night blanketed by a million start with a haloed moon for a pillow;

★ saying "Merry Christmas" early on in December and meaning it for the whole month.

Three Gifts

"Gold is the money of kings, silver is the money of gentlemen, barter is the money of peasants – but debt is the money of slaves." — Norm Franz

Coming through an Eastern Egress they presented the baby with a kingly gift. Every time we lay our true gifts at the foot of the manger, we re-offer ourselves to the one we are proclaiming has the right to rule over our lives. Like the wisemen may we observe obeisance to his Lordship.

"The words which express our faith and piety are not definite; yet they are significant and fragrant like frankincense to superior natures." (Henry David Thoreau) Frankincense was used in worship at the temple in Jerusalem. It was used in thanksgiving and praise gifts to God. The incense gave the meal offerings their pleasant aroma.

Myrrh was another aromatic fragrance. Nicodemus brought a hundred pounds of myrrh and aloes to prepare the body of Jesus for burial after he took Him down from the cross.

Christians like the story of the wise men so much that over the passing years we have added many embellishments to it.

The names, Caspar, Melchior, and Balthazar and their ethnic backgrounds came to the story somewhere between the fifth and seventh centuries. Another piece of added folklore is the number of wise men. The only three in the Bible story is the number of gifts.

Some speculate that the wise men were Zoroastrians from what is present-day Iran, but we don't know that, either. "Wise men" may mean that they were astrologers, who studied the stars.

Then, in the eleventh century, three bodies, which were assumed to be those of the Wise Men, were disinterred in the Holy Land, transported to Cologne, Germany, each in its own ship, to be reburied there. This journey is the source of the Christmas carol, "I Saw Three Ships." We have no way of knowing whose bones were actually reburied.

Just the basic story, without embellishment is both rich and wonderful. We see King Herod and Jerusalem in terror and the wise men's travels commandeered by dreams.

Gold was a medium of exchange more reliable than any country's money in those days. Frankincense and myrrh were sacred spices burned before the altar of the Lord. Myrrh was also associated with marriages and burials. Nicodemus provided a hundredweight (about 75 pounds) of myrrh and aloes for Jesus' burial.

You may be able to find oil of frankincense and myrrh at a specialty shop for the children to smell (or from people who sell candles or candle-making supplies).

The very best gifts are the three gifts of Christ; yesterday, today and tomorrow.

Find Us Hopeful

Loving Lord and Father, help us to remember the birth of Jesus even as we yearn for it and wait upon it. May we once more share in the song of the angels, the gladness of the shepherds and the worship of the wise kings. With a firm slam, close tight the doors of hate that are open around the world. Let kindness flow from every gift and allow good-will to spread with every greeting in whatever space and language from which it is offered.

In this conflicted world may we pause for a moment of peace and find it fulfilling – so much so that we seek to make it our way. In the week ahead, deliver us from evil by the blessing which Christ brings. Then keep us from evil by the peace which passes all understanding.

May Christmas Eve find us hopeful and Christmas morning make us glad to be your children. Then, on Christmas evening, bring us to our beds with transformed thoughts of others and grateful thoughts of you – thoughts of mercy and peace enough to convince us of what you have already done. May we be made both forgiving and forgiven in the name of the babe who will grow to reign and rule and teach us to pray. In his name. Amen.

Surrounded by Gifts

Thornton Wilder, perhaps America's greatest playwright, told a story from 19th Century France which he had heard from one of the persons involved. Apparently, the local custom in a French province held that, on each New Year's Day, one should send flowers to any home to which you had been invited for dinner in the past year. When that day rolled around, one poor young artist did the best he could to honor the tradition with his limited resources. Not having the money to send flowers, he sent paintings of flowers to his hosts.

Most of those who received them wouldn't think of hanging the works of a modest young amateur in their homes. So, many paintings ended up in a back room or tucked away in storage. One family went even farther than that. Soon after the painter moved to Paris, they gathered nearly a dozen paintings they had acquired over the years and burned them, because they were taking up so much space. One of the children in the family told Wilder that's how he helped send 11 potentially major works of the superb impressionist, Paul Cezanne, up in smoke. There is no possible way to estimate the worth of these nearly priceless works, but it was certainly in the millions of dollars. In 2012, Cézanne's painting, *The Card Players,* sold for the most money (at that time) ever paid for any art work - $250 million!

As the Christmas season comes to a close and we enter a New Year, we do so surrounded by gifts of inestimable worth. I wonder ... just how many times have I missed a gift that was within my reach? How often did I pass one by? Worse yet, how often is one of God's masterpieces right in front of my face and I fail to recognize just how precious it is? Jesus is God's ultimate gift, but nothing God makes is without value. I render it useless when I refuse to accept it, use it, learn from it. A red sunset, a peaceful moment before a hectic day hits, an unexpected distraction that yields a beautiful surprise – these and a million other "messages" send Good News my way.

Undecking

It's that time, God. Time for the faithful to come and "undeck the halls." The energy for packing up, Lord, is much less than the excitement around decking the halls with boughs of holly, sprigs of joy and ribbons of rejoicing. All that holiday hope, Heavenly Father, as well as creative Christmas power has now spun a cocoon itself until, once again, we are ready for another ADVENTure. But for now, O Love Made Flesh, we re-pack the crèche. Each figure is nested in its place of safe rest. Move us, Lord, to the next stage of the journey. Children grow up, grapes become wine. A not so young man finds more wrinkles. Life displays its potent changes. Spring is coming, Lord of all time, but it is still far off to those of us following calendar time.

May I ask, Father, for the warmth of a heart that remains wrapped in the manger? In putting away Mary and Joseph, don't let me put away Christmas wonder. While with such care and soft wrapping, I cautiously re-place the shepherds and wise men in their own containers, don't allow me to lose their sense of joy. And awe. And wonder. The animals with silent, adoring eyes, nearly as luminous as the star itself, glowing like their own little halos.

May I seek your Spirit? Where is it? In the wind; the eyes of another; the future? Help me to seek like the wisemen, trust like Mary and Joseph and join with the shepherds in hearing the songs of the angels. That's what it is to find you, isn't it God?

Prayer

May I be Your manger now, Jesus? May I carry You and blanket You with the adoration You deserve but so seldom get? I know that for you, far too soon, will come days of hurt and disappointment and then death. But for now, Lord, just for now, let me worship You as the Lord of All Creation who has become a child. Let me look in awe at the sheer gift of You. Let me be the angel and shepherd, wiseman and star. Let me be Your audience. I won't forget: born in wonder, born of flesh, born through the will of your Father. Born in my heart. I will never forget. In Your name, Father, I will remember. In Your name, Spirit, I will sing and laugh and love. In Your name Jesus, I will pray. Amen.

The Clock Doesn't Tick

Soon it will be midnight, Lord, but the clock isn't ticking. Clocks don't tick anymore. The hands aren't moving toward 12 – nowadays there are precious few clocks that even have hands. But the New Year is approaching anyway. And I'm not nearly done with the old one, Lord. I still have unmet dreams and only partly fulfilled lines on my list of goals. And, oh yes, beside that, I don't really like change anyway.

The year now passing before me, God, was hardly as good as it should have been. The same old shortcomings seemed just as much in evidence on December 31st as they were in the newest part of January. Improvement was scarce, Lord, from principalities and powers all the way down to little old me. But those days are past now, Eternal Timepiece of Creation, and I have to look ahead. First, though, forgive my weaknesses of will and shortcomings of self-awareness. I have hindered the coming of your Kingdom by refusing to recognize it blossoming all around me.

Help me to make the coming year a better one. Lead me in the ways of wonder; the protocols of peace; and the generous gifts of grace. Amen.